Cat Weatherill is a performance storyteller, performing internationally at literature and storytelling festivals, in theatres, and in schools. She loves to travel the world, having adventures and making stories from them.

She lives in England, in a tiny black and white cottage that is four hundred years old.

www.catweatherillauthor.com

Books by Cat Weatherill

Barkbelly
Snowbone
Wild Magic
Jaco the Leek
Famous Me

Published in 2018 by Tansy Books

ISBN 978-1-912009-09-1

Letterpress titles by Francesca Kay francescakay.co.uk
Designed by Matthew Lloyd

CAT WEATHERILL

ZAC and the ZOMBEARDS

To Eoin
Best Wishes!
Cat Weatherill

Tansy Books

CHAPTER 1

I'm walking home from Jamie's house when the screaming begins.

What the…?

The noise is coming from me. I'm like a balloon with the air coming out.

I'm glad I'm on my own.Except I'm not. I've got a dog with me now. A scruffy little brown thing.

'Go away - I didn't call you,' I tell him. 'Get down! Your claws are flamin' sharp.'

What is making this noise?

'Get *down,* dog!'

I pat my chest and arms. The screaming continues. I stamp my feet. Same. I lift my sweatshirt. Nothing looks different. But something makes me press the silver button on my jeans ...

... and the screaming stops. Instantly. The dog sits down. He wags his tail like he's apologising then goes away.

Once I'm home, I go straight to my bedroom and open the wardrobe. I have two pairs of jeans, both the same. They're supermarket cheapies - buy one, get one free. I'm pretty sure the other pair doesn't have a silver button.

I'm right. The button on the other pair is black plastic. But the screamer is silver metal, round, quite thick and has no holes, just a loop to attach it by.

I go to find Mum.

She's in the kitchen, eating yoghurt, talking on the phone and cooking supper all at the same time.

'You'll look great!' she's saying. 'Do it!' She takes another mouthful of yoghurt while she listens. 'Of course you're not too old. Loads of people have pink hair these days.'

She goes to the fridge, takes out the orange juice and fills a glass for me. *'Sal,'* she mouths, and rolls her eyes. Sal is Mum's best friend. When they are together, they behave very badly.

Sometimes I feel like I don't have a mum, she's more like an older sister. We even look alike. We're tall and sporty-looking, with the same dark curly hair and green eyes. We can both bend our thumbs right back.

'Gotta go,' she says. 'Zac is home. Bye. Yes, okay. Bye.' She puts the phone down. 'Right. How are you?'

'Fine. I'm just wondering about something. Where did this come from?' I lift my sweatshirt and show her the button. 'I can't remember,' she says. 'Is it important?'

'Maybe.'

'I was afraid you would say that. I have no idea. Oh *bum.'*

She stares at a blob of yoghurt that has fallen onto her tee shirt. 'Look at this. I'm like a baby. I need a bib.'

She dabs at the mess, making it worse.

'I remember how you lost the old button.'

'I caught it on my bag and ripped it off.'

'Yes.' She opens a bag of pasta while she thinks some more. Then her eyes widen.

'I *can* remember. How scary is that? My life is so dull, I remember where buttons come from. It came from Grampy. I was getting rid of some old clothes for him, and I cut off the buttons. Don't know why I still do that. My mum always did it. *'Save them!' she'd say. 'You might need one, Amy, one day!'*

'Anyway, what's wrong with it? Does it need sewing again?'

'No. I was just wondering.'

I finish my orange juice. 'Can I sleep at Grampy's tonight?'

'Sure.'

Great! I want to solve this one.

CHAPTER 2

Grampy lives on his own, just around the corner. My dad moved out two years ago and I don't get to see him often, so Grampy is important to me. But he is old. He's sixty three and creaky. He doesn't play football and doesn't have a motorbike - things like that. But he is still fun to be with.

I have my own key, so I let myself in. I find him in the living room, dozing in his favourite chair. It's an old leather thing with a dent where his bum fits.

'Grampy?'

He wakes up like an old dog. 'Ohhhh… What time is it?' He yawns, stretches, runs his hands over his head. It's as stubbly as his chin.

'I got too comfy. Dropped off.'

'I've come to ask you something, Grampy. I lost a button off my jeans, so Mum sewed a new one on, and she said it came from you. And just an hour ago, when I was walking home from Jamie's, it started screaming.'

Grampy suddenly sits up straight in his chair and looks right at me.

'Screaming? Like a high-pitched wail?'

'Yes, and -

'There's something amiss, lad.'

'Amiss?'

'Wrong, Zac – wrong. We need to go.'

Grampy puts his hands onto the arms of the chair

and tries to stand up.

'Whoar!' he says, and his bum comes up... and slides back down again.

'Oh, *bottles*.' He slaps the chair and tries harder. His face goes red, his bum lifts… and the chair sucks him back down again.

'Lad,' he says, 'give me a hand or we'll be here till Tuesday. It's like being eaten by a ruddy octopus.'

I give him my hand and haul him to his feet. 'Your legs are too thin, Grampy. There's nothing of you.'

'I know. I need more puddin'. A man needs puddin' to fill out his legs. Right, where's my coat?'

I fetch his coat from the hall. But Grampy shakes his head.

'No, not that one tonight.'

He goes into the hall himself. I follow him, wondering what coat he means. He only has one - hasn't he?

Grampy goes to the door under the stairs and lifts the carpet beside it. Hidden underneath is a long, thin silver key. Grampy slips it into the keyhole: *ckkk*.

He opens the door and steps under the stairs into a cupboard. Well, I *imagine* it's a cupboard. I don't know for sure. I've never been in there. I don't like small spaces, they really freak me out. I got trapped in a wardrobe when I was five and thought I would die. I stay out now.

Grampy passes a black jacket to me.

It's heavy! The jacket seems to have endless pockets, stuffed with... Well, I have no idea what they are stuffed with, but there must be something making the jacket weigh so much.

'We'd best take this too,' says Grampy, and he pulls out what looks like an oxygen tank. A long thin cylinder like divers wear. Grampy puts it down on the floor and goes back into the little room. I hear something being opened and closed. A cupboard or a wooden box? Then Grampy comes out again, with a thin black rubber tube – and a gun.

'What are you doing with *that?* Are you going to shoot someone?'

'Maybe,' he says. 'We need protection, Zac. Things can get nasty. This is a Grade 2 Brassica Blaster. Came all the way from America. You screw this tube into the top, like so… ' he unscrews a cap on the top of the tank and screws the tube on in its place '… then put the tank into the jacket.'

He takes the jacket again and shows me a long pocket on the back with a flap at the top. 'There's a hole inside, see?' He turns the jacket over to show me the lining. 'So we slip the tank into the pocket, fasten this button, then feed the tube through this hole and down the sleeve.'

He pushes till the tube snakes out.

'Now I'll put the jacket on and get fixed up.'

He struggles into the jacket, fishes for the end of the tube and screws it into the base of the gun. 'It works like a water pistol, see? But it's pressurised, so it's far more powerful. It really shoots out strong.'

'But it's just a water gun?'

'Nay, lad, it's not firing water! It's loaded with Brassica Juice. My own special blend of broccoli, sprout and cabbage, all boiled together to make a thick green slop. By heck, it stinks. And they can't stand it. It doesn't kill them, but it really stops them in their tracks. Some howl when they're hit. It stings.'

'Grampy, I don't understand. Who can't stand it? Who are we fighting?'

'Bogles, lubbers, ghouls - anything with a body. It doesn't work with ghosts. Goes right through 'em. Mind you, sprouts go right through me!'

He makes a fart noise. Usually I would laugh, but right now my head is somewhere else.

'Grampy - where are we going?'

'Did I not say?'

'No.'

'To the graveyard, Zac. The graveyard!'

CHAPTER 3

It's dark on the street. There's no moon, just a thick coat of cloud. No one is around. *How brilliant is this?* I thought I'd be watching tv or doing homework tonight. But I'm heading to a graveyard to fight bogles and lubbers - whatever they are.

I know I can do it. I'm always beating Jamie and Joel at games. I always shoot before they do. Ghost hunting! Can't wait to tell them all about it tomorrow. Jamie will roll his eyes like he always does, and say 'Yeah, yeah, right - I believe you.' But how can he, really? You need to be here to understand. Though *I* don't understand everything yet.

'Grampy, are you a ghostbuster?'

Grampy chuckles.

'You could call me that. Though I prefer *Paranormal Peacekeeper* as a job title. That's more what I do. I sort out any problems that arise within the local supernatural community.'

'Are there a lot of problems?'

'No, generally they are a pretty peaceful bunch. But there is trouble now and then. They are no different from the living in that respect.'

'And the Brassica Juice - you said it doesn't kill things?'

'No, it just stops them for a bit. You know like the police? When they use water cannons in a riot? It's like that. It gives us time to get away.' 'Will we need to get away?'

'Maybe. I hope not.'

And the button. Why does it scream?'

'It's an early warning system. It tells you when something supernatural is close by.'

'So this afternoon there was something following me?'

'No. Just close by.'

'What was it?'

'I don't know. But we'll find out soon enough.'

We walk on in the direction of the sea. It doesn't take long from Grampy's house. Five minutes and we're out of the town and into the countryside. Already I can smell the salt in the air.

There are six or seven churches in the town. The one we're going to is my favourite. They call it the Smugglers' Church. It's really old, and there are stories about secret tunnels that begin under the church and go in three directions. One tunnel leads to the beach, another to a pub in the town, and a third to a farmhouse inland. Long ago, when the Customs Men came, the smugglers were able to run into the church and escape. There was a priest who used to be a sailor (or a pirate, more like) and he helped them.

We go along Mermaid Lane. The hedges are high. The trees are skinny and bare, like dead men's bones. As we get nearer to the graveyard, my heart starts hammering in my chest. Yes, it's a steep climb, and Grampy is walking fast on his thin legs. But it's something more than being out of breath. This is fear. Cold, cold fear. I can see the church wall and the tall stone gateposts and the heavy iron gates. Everything is grey, grey, graveyard grey. It feels like my trainers are turning to iron, getting heavier and heavier, like deep-sea divers' boots. I don't want to be here, that's what my body is telling me. *Stop telling stories about how brave you are, Zac. You want to go home.*

Grampy looks serious, like his head is full of thoughts. And he looks younger, as if the years are falling away from him. Where is my old Grampy? This man has energy and a gun in his pocket. His eyes are shining, tiger-bright.

'You need to be quiet when we get in there, lad,' he says. 'No chatting. No questions unless you really need to know. And keep your wits about you. You have eyes and ears. Use them. Concentrate. Don't believe everything you hear. Trust your heart, not the ghoulies. Stay by me. If we get separated - get out, fast as you can.'

I'm starting to feel sick. I'm sweating like a boxer. My legs are moving me forward, but I don't want to go. We reach the graveyard gates.

'Right, in we go,' says Grampy. His hand slides inside his jacket for the Brassica Blaster.

'I can't,' I say, and I stop dead.

'What?'

'I can't go in, Grampy. I...I... just can't.'Grampy looks at me. He puts his hands on my shoulders.

'You have Morgan blood in your veins,' he says, gently but firmly. 'You are braver than you think. You can do this. You're a man now.'

'I'm eleven, Grampy.'

Grampy frowns. 'Eleven? I thought you were thirteen.'

'No. Eleven. You're getting muddled, Grampy.'

I begin to panic. Right now, I need my grandad to be strong and sure, but his brain's gone walkabout.

'I was thirteen when I began this,' says Grampy, in a faraway voice. 'It was raining... Darker than this. Me and Pa together.' He stops. Sighs. 'You'll wait here then? I have to go in, lad. Have to sort this. You'll be okay? I won't be long, I hope.'

He strokes my cheek with a rough finger. 'Another time.'

He opens the gates and slips inside.

I watch him walk up the straight path towards the church. He's stiff in one leg. A bit wonky. Old. But he's brave. He walks up that path like a soldier. Doesn't he have any fear? If he does, he isn't showing it.

I feel worse than ever. I'm scared of the place, the night and what it might be hiding. Of the things that might be in the graveyard, watching me.

But now I feel afraid for Grampy too. Afraid that something might happen to him, and then I will be left alone at the gates, and whatever got Grampy will come for me, and I won't know what to do, and I don't have a Brassica Blaster and... and...

I also feel ashamed of myself. I'm wimping out and I can't believe it. I'm the third oldest in our class. Second tallest. Back in Grampy's house, it sounded exciting. A graveyard at night? Bring it on! Ghosts and ghoulies? Let 'em come!

But now…

My senses are kicking in, trying to help. My ears have grown into satellite dishes, taking in every tiny sound. I can hear the wind whispering through the trees. A farm dog howling. A sheep, coughing in the field behind me. At least, I *hope* it's a sheep. It sounds almost human.

I can smell smoke, drifting across from a farm. Earth, trees, dampness. I can feel the cold, creeping through my trainers into the soles of my feet. Feel the tip of my nose and my ears getting chilled.

But I can't see much, and that is scaring me most of all. The moon is coming and going with the clouds. I can see shapes in the graveyard – crosses, headstones, tombs, statues. But if there are other *things* there too, I can't see them.

Zac, shake yourself. That's what Mum says to me when I'm whinging instead of doing something. So I take my hands out my pockets and shake them, hard. 'You are so rubbish,' I tell myself.

I'm glad my classmates aren't here to see me. Jamie would have gone in, and Joel. Holly Watkins would have been first in, and she is a tiny little thing. But fierce? Whoa! She's like a terrier. I can imagine her in there now, barking at ghosts and snapping at bogles.

While I, Zac Morgan, aged eleven years, three weeks and two days, stand outside the gates shivering like a wet puppy. I've let everyone down – Grampy, the Morgans and me.

And then my jeans start screaming.

CHAPTER 4

I nearly wet myself with fright.

The screaming cuts through the night like a chainsaw. My fingers fly to the silver button and press it hard. The screaming stops. Will Grampy have heard it? Will the ghosts have heard it?

I'm so busy wondering about that, I totally forget what the screaming means.

Something is close. Some thing *is close.*

Oh. My. Willywotsits. What is it?

I look into the blackness. Peer through the iron bars of the gates. Listen like a fox.

Haaaa...

A breath? A sigh? A pant? What? WHAT? I can't tell – but I can hear it.

Haaaaaa…

To my right. It's coming from the right. Isn't it?

Haaaaaaa…

Where is it? What is it?

Haaaaaa.... Haaaa....

Without knowing why, I turn my head and look down the road. The thing that is making the sound isn't in the graveyard at all. It is crawling along the wall – and it is coming right for me.

It looks like a cat except it has no fur. And it is bigger than a cat. Fatter. Its head is round, like a huge pickled onion. Its nose is long and stabbing, like a beak, and its eyes are like human eyes – wide and round with huge black centres.

I don't know which way to turn. If I run ahead there's nothing but fields, and maybe the thing can run – fast. Like a spider. I can't run back to town – that would mean running past it.

There's only one way to go. Into the graveyard.

I go up the path Grampy took. Halfway along, I stop and turn. The cat-thing is following me. It is crawling like a toad. Its whole body sways from side to side as it thrusts one leg forward then the other. But boy, it is fast! Time to RUN.

The path ends at the church. Left? Right? I have no idea which way Grampy went. I choose left and fly round the side of the building, deeper into shadow. Oh, why is it cloudy tonight?

I imagine the cat-thing behind me, licking its lips, blinking those terrible human eyes and breathing hard: *haaaa... haaaaa..... haaaa.*

Then across the graveyard, I see shapes, outlined against the dark sky. People. Four or five of them. Grampy? I run towards them. They hear me and turn. One disappears instantly. Just *vanishes* into thin air! But one steps forward.

'Zac? What's wrong, lad?'

I grab Grampy's arm and point. The cat-thing comes out of the shadows. Its tongue is hanging down. Its eyes are wild and hungry-looking.

'Go on with you, Spyker,' says Grampy to the thing. 'There's nothing here for you. He's with me.'

The thing blinks once, twice, then moves closer.

'Spyker?' growls Grampy. He puts his hand into his jacket and pulls out the Brassica Blaster.

The thing stops. Hisses. Turns and disappears back into the shadows.

'Well, gentlemen,' says Grampy, 'I think it's time I was going anyway. Thank you for this. I will get back to you tomorrow night, okay?'

I stare at the 'gentlemen'. They are ghosts – all of them. One is tall and extremely thin, with a face that looks like it's carved out of white cheese. The second is tall too, dressed in a black suit, very smart, with a black top hat. But the suit looks wet and is grimy with soil. The third is a short man, with stringy white hair and wire spectacles. He doesn't look well. None of them do. That's why they are dead.

'Do not fail us,' says the ghost in the top hat. It comes out like an order, but I hear the worry behind it.

'I won't, Jonathan,' says Grampy. He puts his hand on the ghost's arm, and he seems to know exactly how to do that, because it doesn't sink in or pass right through. 'Tomorrow.'

The ghost nods. Grampy moves his hand to my shoulder and together we walk down the path, back to the graveyard gates.

Grampy says nothing. I wait for two minutes but that is all I can manage. I have to know. 'Did you find out what the problem is, Grampy? Is it bad?'

'Very bad,' says Grampy. 'It's ZOMBEARDS!'

CHAPTER 5

'What are *zombeards?*'

Grampy stops and fishes in one of the many pockets in his jacket. He pulls out a white paper bag. 'Humbug?'

'GRAMPY!' I'm going to explode with curiosity. BANG! There will be bits of me dripping from the trees.

Grampy pops a humbug into his mouth, sucks hard and walks on. 'A zombeard is exactly what it sounds like. It's a zombie with a beard. But they have a brain that still works. This makes them dangerous. Regular zombies are dim creatures. They wander round moaning and looking for things to eat. Dogs, sheep, people... They don't care as long as it's meat. We've only ever had one here. He fell off the end of the cliff on the very first night he came, and that was the end of him. Great daft fool!

But zombeards can still think and talk. They're clumsy – I guess it isn't easy to walk in a dead body! But the main problem is their anger. They are dead but not happy about it. So they cause trouble. And they are hard to stop. They don't listen to reason, so you can't talk to them. And you can't kill a dead man.'

'But you said one fell off the cliff. Didn't that 'kill' him?'

‘In a way. If a zombie falls into the sea, he swallows water. His brain doesn’t stop him doing it. Eventually he sinks. But a zombeard... Not so easy.’

We have reached the end of Mermaid Lane. We turn into Water Street. A black cat runs across our path with a fish’s head in its mouth.

I press on. ‘So now there are zombeards in the graveyard?’ Grampy is being so slow in telling me things.

‘Not exactly. Jonathan - the man with the top hat? He thinks they may be hiding somewhere on the beach. Three of them.’

‘And what do they want?’

‘A girl,’ says Grampy. ‘She’s called Shannon Price, and she is living as a ghost in the graveyard. I was told she had been settling in nicely. But now these zombeards want to turn her into a zombie and take her away. It’s a complicated story. They all died together in a car crash, two weeks ago. The driver had been drinking. They hit a tree and it was all over. Shannon was buried here, but the guys came from Rockport - just down the coast, you know? So they were buried there. But now they have come here.’

‘I don’t understand,’ I say. ‘If they all died together, why is she a ghost and not a zombeard?’

‘Good question, lad. You see? You were born to do this work! You usually get a zombie because someone makes one with a voodoo spell. But some dead people have a virus in their brain. These three guys are brothers. They must have the zombeard virus in them. Simple as that. But Shannon is not related to them, so she became a ghost, not a zombie.'

We have reached Grampy's house. He stops at the gate and starts to search for his key. His jacket has so many pockets, it's like finding a flea on a dog.

'Grampy, I'm sorry.'

'What, lad?'

'I'm sorry. I let you down.' Grampy stops searching. 'No, Zac, it was my fault. I expected too much of you, too soon.'

'But I thought I could do it, Grampy. I wanted to do it.'

'Well you did, in a way. You went in.'

'Only because the cat-thing made me. I was *scared*.' I hang my head. It's feeling too heavy to hold up.

'There's no shame in being scared, Zac. You can't find courage until you feel fear. Tonight wasn't an end – it was a beginning. You'll see.'

But I'm not listening. My Big Adventure ended in failure, falling apart like cheap shoes. I'm a coward. A wimpy kid. I just want to crawl into bed and forget all about it.

CHAPTER 6

I don't feel any better the next day. In fact I feel worse, because as I walk to school, I remember what Grampy said to the ghosts: 'I will get back to you tomorrow.'

But Grampy said nothing to *me* about going back to the graveyard.

When I enter my classroom, Mr Carter is already taking the register. Mr Carter is what my Nana B would call a Gentleman. He's very brainy. He should be teaching in a university or something, so I don't know why he is in a school, teaching us. He even looks like a professor. Or a poet. He's tall and thin, always smart, with long hair that he sweeps back from his face. He wears the same shoes every day. They are black suede pull-on boots. He says they're called Chelsea boots, but I can't imagine the team ever wear them. He's quiet. Not very good at controlling us. If he were an animal, he'd be a hedgehog, curling into a ball when trouble comes. He lets us call him Mr C.

I like him. He's fair and kind, and I like the way he knows things and wants to share the knowledge with us. He gets over-excited sometimes, like a boy on Christmas morning. But he's not a boy. He's twenty eight. He told us.

'Sanjit.'

'Here, Mr Carter.'

'Chloe.'

'Here, Mr Carter.'

'Zac. Zac...? Ah, here you are. Just in time.'

He smiles. I go to my seat. Jamie waves at me across the room. Jamie is my best mate. He's the tallest boy in the class and builds up his arm muscles using his dad's weights. You must never touch his hair. It takes him ages to do it every morning.

'Right,' says Mr Carter. 'As usual on a Tuesday, it's English to begin.'

There's a groan from the back of the classroom. I turn round. Holly Watkins has her head in her hands, so I can't see her face, just two dark plaits.

'I know, Holly. But we have to do it. And because winter is coming, with its long, dark nights, and we have Hallowe'en on Friday, I thought it might be fun to look at ghost stories.'

Yes! Jamie punches the air. Ghost stories! Now we're all listening. Especially me. I might learn something useful here.

'I confess – I am a big fan of ghost stories,' Mr Carter goes on. 'I even write my own. Sometimes, after dark, I will sneak into the graveyard for a bit of inspiration. I love the silence and the shadows. The owls flying by on bone-white wings.'

He blushes, pleased at his own words.

'Have you ever seen a ghost, Mr C?' asks Holly. She has no time for poetry.

'No, I haven't,' Mr Carter admits. 'So I cannot say whether they exist or not. But I can say this: there is a fine tradition of ghost story writing in this country. Some of the most famous writers in the English language wrote ghost stories. William Shakespeare, for example. *Hamlet* sees the ghost of his dead father. *Macbeth* is haunted by Banquo's ghost – Banquo is a man he murdered. Charles Dickens wrote a very famous ghost story, set at Christmas. What is it called?'

Hettie Shaw's hand shoots up first. It always does.

'Hettie?'

'*A Christmas Carol*.'

'Indeed. And the ghosts are...? Yes, Narinder.'

'The Past, the Present and the Future.'

'Indeed they are. So you can see, there's a great tradition here. And we are going to follow in it, by writing ghost stories of our own. I know some of your parents might hear that idea and throw up their hands in horror, if you pardon the pun! But if it was good enough for Dickens, it is certainly good enough for us. And ghost story writing requires one of the things we have already been looking at this term: descriptive writing. Ghost stories are all about creating a spooky atmosphere.'

'And lots of blood,' says Jamie.

Mr Carter shakes his head.

'That's not needed at all! That's just the movies, Jamie. Saturday night popcorn stuff! No, give me a book of the *old* ghost stories, with lots of atmosphere, and I am much happier.

Now, let's look at the shape of ghost stories...'

The lesson flies by. I don't hear half of what Mr C says. My head is full of ghosts, ghoulies and zombeards. Can't wait to see Grampy again.

CHAPTER 7

When I get home, I follow Mum round the house like a puppy, hoping she will suddenly say: 'Pack your jimjams, Zac – you're sleeping at Grampy's.' But she doesn't. She goes on and on about a sick dog she has nursed all day. Mum works for an animal charity, and usually I like to hear her stories. But not today. Today it makes me feel worse, because she is brave without even trying. She sees terrible things and faces up to horrible people who have been cruel to their pets. She is bold and strong and fights for what she believes in.

What would she say if she knew how useless her son had been last night?

And I've been wondering - why doesn't *she* work with Grampy? Maybe she used to, when she was younger. I can't ask. Grampy might be working for the government or something. Like a spy. Top Secret. So I'll have to keep my mouth shut until I know more. I won't talk to Mum, Jamie, *anyone* about it. I don't want to land Grampy in trouble. There's enough of that in the graveyard.

I go to bed at nine o'clock, but just lie there in the dark, thinking. I keep the curtains open, gaze at the sky and try to picture what Grampy is doing.

It's not enough. I'm too restless. So I climb out of bed and look out of the window. The garden is a box of shadows. But I imagine the gate at the far end is opening… and there are figures. Dark figures, three of them. *The zombeards!* They lumber over the lawn, coming towards the house. They look up at my window, craning their necks for a better view. Then one moves closer and the security light comes on. The zombeards shrink back but don't run. They stay just beyond the reach of the light and stand there, swaying on their feet. Watching. Looking. At me.

I don't move. I know they aren't really here – it is just my imagination, making them up. But I wish my head would tell my heart. It feels like someone is kicking a football against the inside of my chest.

The zombeards are a strange gang. I can see them as if they really are down there. They are tall and dressed in ordinary clothes – jeans, jackets, boots. But no caps or beanie hats. Instead they have long, thick hair, down to their shoulders. Their beards reach to their *belly-buttons,* thick and dirty and tangled, more like sheep fleece than hair. How can this be? The brothers have only been dead two weeks. My imagination is going too far! But it feels right. And between the hair and the beards are the eyes. I can't see them, but I know they are seeing me.

Now I feel cold, and it isn't because I'm out of bed in the middle of the night. This is the kind of cold that creeps up your spine like a spider, slowly, slowly, until it steals your breath and seizes your heart. The zombeards are so unnerving. The way they sway, like they are on the deck of a moving ship. The way their arms hang limp by their sides, but their fingers curl and uncurl over and over and over again. The way their mouths hang open, while their blue tongues roll in and out, wetting their bottom lips and dribbling into the beards.

I think of the girl they want, Shannon. She's probably a grown woman. Any woman under forty is a girl to Grampy. Whatever age she is, I don't like the thought of her being carried off by these three. How would they do it, anyway? They can't capture a ghost.

Grampy said they wanted to make her into a zombie.

Suddenly I realise what they are planning to do.

They're going to dig up her body.

And Grampy is going to try stopping them? On his own? With sprout water? Is he mad?

They were strong young men when they were alive. Will they be weak now? No. Those curling fingers are itching to fight. It will be three against one, and Grampy is an old man, skinny as a scarecrow.

For the millionth time, I wish I had been braver last night. But it's too late now. He's gone without me. He's facing them alone.

CHAPTER 8

I sleep badly and and wake up feeling like a donkey has kicked me all over.

'Have you heard from Grampy?' I ask Mum, as I arrive in the kitchen. She's searching in the cupboard for something.

'No. But I'm sure he's fine.'

'But if haven't heard from him, how can you be sure?'

She catches the worry in my voice like a frog catches a fly and turns to look at me, the jar of peanut butter forgotten in her hand.

'Why are you so worried all of a sudden?'

I shrug. 'No reason.'

She doesn't believe me. 'Where is this coming from? Has someone died? Someone's grandad - at school?'

'Mum, the toast. The toast is burning.'

'It doesn't matter, Zac. It's only toast. Having you happy is what matters. You know you can always talk to me about these things, don't you?'

'I'm okay, Mum. I just want the toast. I need to get to school.' I can call at Grampy's house on the way, if I eat quick.

'Okay,' says Mum. She returns to the toaster and slips new bread into it. 'If you're sure.'

How can I tell her what I'm thinking? That Grampy could be lying dead in the graveyard, or worse. The zombeards could have thrown him into the sea, or thrown him from the cliffs – anything.I wish I had a phone of my own! Then I could text him myself. But Mum says I can't have one till I move up to the big school.

Mum passes me the fresh toast and the peanut butter. I spread it on thick and start crunching. I eat it super-fast then grab my jacket and am out of the house before Mum can say anything more.I race down our road and then, instead of going straight on to school, I turn right and head for Grampy's house. I have to run or I'll be late for school. I get to Grampy's hot and panting. I pull off my jacket as I walk up the path. Then I see something. The curtains are still drawn in the downstairs room.

My heart stops.

'Grampy?'

I ring the bell. Wait. *Come on, come on.*

He doesn't come.

I step back and look up at his bedroom window. The curtains are drawn there too. No...!I ring the bell again. Come *on*, Grampy. Answer!

But still – nothing. So now I am frantic, wondering what on earth has happened in the night.

'Hey Zac – you coming?'

I turn. It's Holly Watkins, standing by the gate. She lives in this road too. 'Soon. Just going to wait for my grandad a bit.'

'I'll tell them you're coming, if you're late,' she says, and walks on.

I ring the bell again. Try to get through the side gate, but it's locked. Then I hear whistling. It's Grampy, coming along the road!

'Where have you been?' I say, like I'm his mum and he's a teenager. 'Have you been out all night?'

He nods. 'I'm ready for my bed, I can tell you! It was a good night, though. Worth it. I saw them.'

'Really?'

'Yes. Well, two of them. On the beach after dark.'

'What where they like? Did you get close? Did they see you?'

Grampy holds up his hands to stop me.

'Too many questions for a tired man! And you have school. You'll be late. Go on, get going.'

'Can I come by afterwards? Please?'

He nods. 'Later. Later!'

CHAPTER 9

Grampy is making Brassica Juice when I arrive at his house. He opens the front door and the smell punches me in the face like an angry kangaroo. My eyes start to water. What a stink! The whole house reeks of boiled cabbage and broccoli.

'What happened last night?' I say, as soon as I can breathe properly.

'I could ask you the same question,' says Grampy. 'Poor Joe. Scary for him.'

'He's okay now. What *happened*, Grampy? You said you saw the zombeards?'

'Yes. Down on the beach. Two of them. Jonathan was right. They are hiding out in one of the caves.'

'Did they see you?'

'No, luckily. I kept well back.'

'So what were they doing?'

'Playing cricket.'

'*What?*' He laughs.

'Disappointed, are you? Were you expecting them to be eating someone's brains?'

'No, but... *cricket?!*'

Grampy chuckles. 'They never show that in the horror movies! But like I told you the other day, zombeards are different. They still have brains. So I guess they were doing what they would do if they were still alive. Killing time, playing cricket with a bit of wood and a stone for the ball.'

'But what about the other one?'

'Ah...' Grampy's eyes darken. 'Now *he* is the troublemaker. The dangerous one. He was at the graveyard. Anderson, he's called. Anderson Bell. He's the oldest brother. I went online today and read all about the accident. I'll show you in a minute. Anyways, I didn't see him. He was gone by the time I arrived. But Jonathan - you do remember Jonathan, don't you? The ghost with the top hat? He said Anderson had been smashing up gravestones and demanding to see the girl, Shannon.'

I think about her for a moment. I know she's dead, so they can't hurt her or anything. But it can't be nice, being chased when you want a peaceful new life – or whatever it is ghosts have. And I don't like to think of the graveyard getting smashed up. It's a special place, full of history.

'He must be stopped,' I say. 'They *all* must be stopped. What are you going to do, Grampy?'

'I'm not going to do anything,' he says. '*We* will be doing it – you and me together.'

'*What?*' I feel that cold fear again. 'But I wimped out the other night. Couldn't handle it.'

'Doesn't mean you'll wimp out again. We all have to learn. You want another go, don't you?'

Do I? I don't know. Maybe it's enough just to listen to Grampy. To hear the story, not do it myself.

But how can I let him do it alone? He struggles to put his socks on in the morning. How can he fight three strong zombeards on his own?

'I... think so,' I hear myself saying.

'Good lad,' says Grampy. 'You are a true Morgan. Brave and bold!' He claps his hands together and rubs them. 'Right! Let's get started. You can read the newspaper articles online, and I'll phone your mum to tell her you're stopping over tonight. Then you can nip home, fetch your night things and some warm clothes. Wear your other pair of jeans. We don't want the alarm button going off tonight. Come back and we'll eat something. Then we'll head out about ten o'clock. Does that sound like a plan?'

I nod. It's only later, when I'm heading back home for my clothes, that I realise: Grampy still hasn't said what he – no, what *we* are going to do!

CHAPTER 10

Ten o'clock comes. I've read the online newspaper articles about the car crash. I've eaten a sausage sandwich. I've been to the toilet four times but think I need to go again.

Grampy has filled the Brassica Blaster with fresh juice – if 'fresh' is the right word to use for such poisonous gunk. Now he straps it on.

'Ready, lad?'

I swallow hard and nod. Put my scarf on, just to have something to do. Grampy opens the door and we step out into another world. Well, that's how it looks. Everything is blue. Lunar blue. There's a full moon and a deep frost. There are shadows behind every tree, sharp as comet tails.

We head to the Smugglers' Church. It doesn't take long. When we get there Spyker, that strange bald cat-thing, is squatting on the wall near the gate. He looks like a gargoyle, one of those old stone carvings on the church.He doesn't move as we pass by. Just stares at us with eyes as silver as spoons.

As we go up the path, a ghost steps out of the shadows in the church porch. Tall, thin, long coat – it's Jonathan.

'Any sign of 'em?' whispers Grampy.

'Not yet. But it's early. Past midnight is more usual.'

‘Hmm. Where’s Shannon?’

‘Up in the bell tower with Barton and McAndrew.’

‘Right then. We’ll wait beneath the yew. Plenty of cover there.’

There are many yew trees in the graveyard, but one is bigger than all the rest. It’s ancient – over a thousand years old. It was here before the church was even built. The branches spread out on every side and sweep down to touch the ground. It’s like hiding under an enormous green skirt. Grampy has chosen well. There’s no frost under the tree, the branches keep the wind out, and we have a good view of the graveyard. The time creeps by like a toad. I am losing contact with my toes. Boy, it’s cold. Eleven o’clock comes. The church bell rings the hour. An owl abandons the tower. It flies past us, its wings as white as winter. *Haha!* Mr Carter would like that simile! I must remember to use it in my ghost story.

We keep sitting.

Nearly midnight. Grampy reaches into a pocket and pulls out a slim silver container.

What is it? Some kind of zombie detector? A booby trap to blow off zombie feet? A time portal?

Grandad unscrews the top and the smell of tomato soup drifts into the chilly air.

‘What?’ he says, seeing my disappointed face. ‘A man needs to keep his strength up. This will keep the cold out for a while longer.'

He pours some soup into the cup and offers it to me. I shake my head. How can he think of eating at a time like this?

The church bell starts to strike midnight. I remember Jonathan's words and want the toilet again. The Bell brothers will be coming. They will be on the beach right now, out of their cave, climbing up the cliff path on heavy legs, feet dragging over the gravel. They are coming, coming, coming...Grampy's head suddenly tilts to one side like a dog's. He frowns. I think my heart is going to punch its way out of my chest. He finishes the soup and screws the lid back onto the flask. He raises his eyes and nods at me, saying nothing.

I don't need him to speak. I know what this means. THEY'RE HERE.

CHAPTER 11

I hear them before I see them. There's a deep voice, muttering something. A second voice mumbles a reply.

I peer through the branches. Nothing. Then they arrive, coming from behind us. They lurch along the path, swaying from side to side like they're trying to walk onboard a rolling ship. The night turns even colder. My breath is hanging in front of me like a ghost.

I can see them clearly. They look like the photos I saw online. Anderson, the oldest brother, is the tallest and strongest looking.

He's deathly pale, almost blue in the moonlight. His beard is sandy blond and hanging down to his belly-button. He's dressed in a long navy blue coat, with jeans underneath and boots. Was he buried like that? In a coat? No... He must have stolen it or found it somewhere. On a scarecrow by the look of it. It's covered with mud.

His brothers look filthy too. One is in baggy jeans, the other in tracksuit bottoms. Both wear trainers, puffy jackets and caps. Jaden Bell, the middle brother, is dark-haired. His beard is like a scrap of black fur stuck onto his chin. It doesn't look real, but it is.

Nic Bell is the youngest. He's thin, with arms that seem too long for his body. His beard is matted and tangled, the colour of toffee. He was the one driving the car when it crashed. The online articles said he had been drunk, and the car skidded off the road and hit a wall at 'an unforgivable speed.' Shannon was Anderson's girlfriend. Jaden was just along for the ride. He was the quiet one, according to the reports.

And now here they are. Very dead and bearded.

'SHANNON!' Anderson's voice chainsaws through the night. 'SHANNON!'

All three of them are scanning the graveyard, their eyes glowing like lanterns.

'SHANNON!'

Grampy rises to a crouch beside me. How long is he going to wait before tackling them? I still haven't heard of any plan.

'Go away, Andy. I want nothing more to do with you. With any of you.'

Shannon's voice drifts on the wind like smoke. Instantly, the zombeards look up to the bell tower.

'You're coming with us,' calls Anderson.

'I'm never going anywhere with you again, Anderson Bell. It was going with you that led me here. I should be at home, watching tv, not dead in a graveyard, drifting round like something from Harry Potter.'

'You're coming with us,' says Anderson again. I feel like shouting at him: 'Get over it! Move on!' But I don't.

Anderson's eyes seem to glow brighter than ever. Then he turns and lurches away, with the others following him. He goes towards the far side of the graveyard. The newer bit. The place where people these days are buried.'

No...' growls Grampy.

I stand up for a better view. Even from here, I can see what Anderson is planning. He drops to his knees and starts digging into one of the graves. Digging with both hands, like a dog burying a bone. Except he's not going to put something into the ground. He's going to take something – someone – out of it.

'Nooooo!' Shannon screams down from the bell tower roof. 'Don't you dare. Don't you DARE!'

Now Grampy is on his feet, flipping a switch on the Brassica Blaster, pushing his way out from under the tree and half-running towards the zombeards.

'Grampy – no!'

But he's gone. Gone, gone, gone, and I'm still here, watching him go, doing nothing. How rubbish is that? But I'm so terrified, I just can't move. I CAN'T MOVE. I don't know how Grampy is doing it.

Grampy is up to full speed now. 'Leave her be!' he shouts. 'You heard what she said. Be off or I'll shoot.'

But they aren't going anywhere. Jaden and Nic

start to laugh. Anderson is still digging behind them.

'Shoot away, Grampa!' sneers Nic, and he waves his hands like he's firing two pistols: *Puuw! Puuw! Puuw!*

VOOOSH! Grampy opens fire with full force. Jaden is knocked backwards off his feet. He falls on top of Anderson, who roars and shoves him off. Jaden writhes on the ground, shouting, shouting. Nic swears as Grampy turns the force on him. The Brassica Juice is like liquid dragon, green and fiery. Nic howls as the juice stings his face, his hands, his eyes. He's half-blinded, staggering now. He bangs a knee hard on a headstone and howls in pain. *So they can feel pain?* I'll remember that.

Grampy is still marching forward, like an action movie hero, spraying them and shouting, 'Take that, you dead fools!' He's unstoppable.

Anderson has stopped digging. He's getting to his feet. He's towering over Grampy and yes, Grampy is spraying, but Anderson is taking the pain. I can see the juice running down his face, dripping off his beard, soaking his clothes, but he doesn't care. He's the unstoppable one now.

He rushes at Grampy and swipes him with his fist. Knocks him sideways, like he's no more than a child, and Grampy goes down. He twists in the air as he falls and lands heavily, with the Blaster tank half under him, while his head snaps forwards and hits a half-sunken headstone.

He doesn't move.

But I do.

I'm out from under the tree and running to help Grampy. Then everything starts happening at once. Anderson is digging again, there's a scream behind me, and the ghost of Shannon Price flies past and arrives at the grave before I do. She's howling, wailing, flying round the heads of Jaden and Nic like a demon. They're trying to bat her away. Nic even has a piece of wood. And there's so much chaos and craziness, they don't notice me, in the shadow of the headstone, desperately trying to wake Grampy up and get him away to safety.

Now there are ghosts coming to help Shannon. Jonathan, Cheese Face and Shorty coming from the church. Other rising up out of the ground. But they can't do anything. There's nothing to them. Their hands pass right through the zombeards. They can't hold weapons and the zombeards know that.

Nic is starting to walk away now, bored by it all. Jaden is wavering, looking from one brother to the other, trying to decide – stay or go.

Now Anderson starts howling, triumphantly, like a wild dog. He's head down in the grave, lying flat on his belly. The soil is flying everywhere. There's a terrible sound of wood being hammered and ripped. Then a coffin lid is thrown into the air. Tossed as easy as a pancake. *How strong is this guy*? He leans even further down into the grave, while Shannon screams like a banshee: *NOOOOOOOOOO!*

I don't know what Anderson does. I can't see. But suddenly Shannon's ghost disappears.

Everything falls silent.

Anderson pushes himself upright. He's covered in soil, like a human mole. His beard is caked with it. But he is grinning. Jaden is staring. Nic comes back and laughs, once.

And out of the grave climbs Shannon Price, looking as perfect as can be.

She's not a mouldy corpse, with bones showing and bits dropping off. She doesn't even have any car-crash injuries. There's no blood on her. But her face... *aiee.*

It's the expression. There's nothing there. No warmth, no fear, no nothing. Her eyes are dark, like two polished pebbles. She looks around slowly, as if she's trying to understand where she is and what's happened. But still her face shows nothing.

Then Anderson takes hold of her hand and roughly leads her away, across the graveyard, heading back towards the beach. As they go, she suddenly turns her head and looks right at me. Her eyes seem to clear, she opens her mouth and breathes two words: *'Save me.'* I feel my heart break in two - it's terrible to see.

Then they're gone, and I'm sitting there with Grampy, cradling his body to mine, hoping and praying he will open his eyes when something *TOUCHES* me on the shoulder.'

AAAARGH!'

I spin around, expecting some new horror.

It's Mr Carter.

CHAPTER 12

'What are you doing here?' I say. I mean – you don't expect to bump into your teacher in a graveyard in the middle of the night, do you? But I guess he wasn't expecting to bump into *me.*

'Getting inspiration,' he says. 'I told you the other day, I come here to get ideas for stories.'

'Did you see what happened?'

'No? I saw some people walking away as I came around the corner, but that was it. Did they attack him?'

'Not really. It's complicated.'

Suddenly Grampy moves a bit and opens his eyes.

'Zac? Are you alright, lad?'

'Don't you worry about me, Grampy! How are you?'

'Dizzy, if I'm being honest.' He struggles to get up. 'Have they gone?'

'Yes. And they took Shannon with them.'

'Oh no...' He struggles more.

'Hold on there, Mr ....?'

'Morgan,' I say.'

'Mr Morgan, you've had a nasty knock to the head. There's blood - see? You need to go to the hospital to be checked. I'll call an ambulance.' Mr C fishes in a pocket for his phone.'

'No! No ambulance. If that comes, the police will come, and there'll be all kinds of questions asked.

We're trying to keep this quiet.'

'It's alright, Grampy, it's alright!' He's wriggling like a tadpole. We can hardly hold him down. '*No ambulance,'* I tell Mr C.'

Okay,' he says. 'But I'll walk home with you both. Make sure he gets there.'

'Brilliant,' I say, and I'm on my feet and heading after the zombeards before he can stop me.

'Zac! Where are you going?'

'I have things to do! Get him home for me. Thank you!'

And with that, I disappear into the shadows.

CHAPTER 13

I go through the gate beside the church, as the zombeards did. It leads to the sea, across the fields. But first there's a skinny path, overgrown with brambles. I don't want to go down it but I have to. I start walking. The trees almost meet at the top, so I lose the moon, but I fix on a patch of deep blue at the far end. The way out.

The brambles catch at my clothes. There are nettles too. I feel my hand get stung as I hurry on. But the blue patch is coming closer. Nearly there.

I come out into the moonlight again. I can see two rough paths across the field, cutting through the endless rows of cabbages. One leads to the sea. The other leads to Cold Wall Farm. The farmer there has cows. Huge herds of them. Sometimes they're in the fields, but not tonight. There's nothing moving tonight. No cows, no zombeards, nothing.

DOOF! Something slams into me from behind. An arm wraps around my middle, a hand covers my mouth. I smell salt water and damp cloth. Unwashed flesh and beery breath. I struggle hard and manage to look over my shoulder. It's Nic Bell, with his too-long arms, smothering me like an octopus, and he is strong. SO strong. I can't get free. I can't shout. I can't *breathe*.

I start kicking him, backwards, over and over.

He can feel it. He groans and holds on tighter. I gather all my energy, lean back against him, lift *both* feet of the ground and kick him like a donkey.

He roars, and his grip loosens for a second, just long enough for me to wriggle free. I drop through his arms and start racing away across the fields, towards the farm.

But he is following me. I can hear his boots slamming the hard earth path, and his heavy breathing. And now, up ahead, I see something coming in from the right, heading diagonally. I can't see what it is, but it's cutting through the cabbages like a missile, deadly fast. Closer, closer closer

'*YEOWWW!*'

Spyker flies up from the ground and lands on Nic. There's a howl of pain as twenty razor-sharp claws dig in to his still-soft flesh. I slow for a moment, turn and see the zombeard fighting with the bald cat. Spyker has hold of his beard. He's spitting and snarling, biting at Nic's hand as he tries to pull him off. But then Nic grabs Spyker by the scruff of the neck, rips him off and hurls him back into the cabbages.

I don't hang around. I start running again, fast as I can, heading for the farm. I can see the wall now, the one that goes all around and gives the place its name. I don't care if it's cold or not – I'm going over it.

I arrive so fast, I slam into it. It almost knocks the breath out of my body, but I grab hold and start to climb. It's high, over two metres, but easy. It's old. There are jagged bits sticking out everywhere. I scramble up like a rat, throw one leg over and pause to catch my breath.

Nic is still coming. He's nearly at the wall when Spyker flies at him again. He lands on the zombeard's thigh and bites down hard. Nic howls so loud, they must hear it in town. Or on the beach.

I can't think about that now.

I pull up my other leg and look beyond the wall. It's a huge yard, full of cows. There are dozens of them, massive things, mostly standing up. Cows can be dangerous in a herd. They can crush you against a wall. If you fall over, they can trample you to death. I don't want to go in with them, but there's nowhere else to go.

I'm gonna risk it.

I look down. *No!* There's a huge pile of cow manure right below. A mountain of stinking filth. I'm going to be *covered* in it. But it will break the fall.

I drop down from the wall, straight into it. *Eurgh!* It has a dry crust, but underneath it's liquid: thick, brown and totally foul. I'm in it up to my waist.

I start to push my way out. I stumble - I can't help it - and my hands reach out to stop myself falling. So now I have it up to my elbows too, and the smell is unholy.

The cows have noticed. They turn and watch me. Some start to come over - cows are super-curious. Slowly, slowly I drag myself out of the dirt heap. It seems to go on forever. Step by filthy step… The evil stuff drags at me like quicksand. But I do it. I come out dripping, looking like some monster from Hell. The cows move back, warily. I decide to go around them, not through them. If I follow the wall, I should come to a door or something.

There's a scrambling sound behind me and a brick falls. I turn. Nic is climbing over the wall. His eyes are amber. He sees me, grins, and hauls the rest of his body onto the top of the wall. Then he stands up, like some triumphant soldier, fixes those terrible eyes on me and just stares. Then he jumps down, right off the wall, pencil-straight and easy, like he's jumping into a swimming pool.

He lands in the manure, like I did. He begins to push his way out of it, like I did.

Except he stops after just two strides. He looks down, puzzled. He holds up his mucky hands and stares at them.

He is melting! The manure is melting him like a candle!

Nic's expression changes from puzzlement to anger. He roars, and waves his arms, but that unbalances him. He tumbles backwards into the muck heap and - *shloop.* It sucks him down. Down, down, down. I hear one last cry and then - nothing. It's like he's never been there at all.

The cows turn away. Game over.

Spyker is on the wall, his hairless skin shining silver in the moonlight. He looks like he's smiling.

I clamber back up.

'Good job,' purrs Spyker, and I almost fall off the wall. I never dreamed he could speak. 'Go home now. Sleep.'

Sleep? After everything I have seen tonight, I don't think I'll ever sleep again.

CHAPTER 14

'Don't get so upset, Zac. You did a great job, and on your own too. I'm proud of you.'

It's 4.15 in the morning, we're eating fried egg sandwiches in Grampy's kitchen, I've killed a zombie and have to go to school in a few hours. This is unreal.

'Proud of me?'

'There's one less zombeard to fight now, thanks to you.'

'But I killed a man, Grampy! He is *dead* because of me.'

Grampy puts down his sandwich and wipes his mouth. 'Zac, you're getting a bit confused here. Two things… First: technically speaking, you can't kill a zombeard. He's already dead and you can't kill a dead man. Second: *you* didn't kill him. The muck heap did that. And answer me this: when you chased after them, what did you think you would do when you found them? Tell them off? Nic would have killed you. Remember that.'

'But it's *hard*, Grampy. He was real. He wasn't something from a computer game. He was Nic Bell.'

'Not anymore, he wasn't. Believe me, Zac. The real Nic Bell had long gone, with just a few deep-wired habits remaining, like trailing after his brothers and playing cricket. But everything good that makes us human - all the love and kindness and caring - that wasn't in him anymore, I promise you.'

I stare at my plate. I don't know what to say.'

You have to get your head round this,' says Grampy. 'Go to bed now. It will seem clearer in the morning.'

But it doesn't. I walk to school as if I'm sleepwalking. My head is spinning.

As I enter the classroom, Mr Carter stares at me, clearly relieved. But he doesn't say anything, simply nods and I take my seat.

'You look rougher than the bottom of a parrot's cage,' whispers Joel.

Joel is my second best friend in the class. He's keeps guinea pigs, has family in Jamaica and always shares his sweets. He slips me a toffee right now and grins. 'Did you go clubbing last night?'

'No sleep,' I manage to say.

'Yeah. I believe you.' He winks.

The morning passes. Maths, history… I don't really care. My head is elsewhere.

Then it's lunchtime. As we are clearing away our books, Hettie Shaw says, 'Mr C, have you made your costume?'

'Yes, I have,' he replies. 'Though you will have to wait till tonight, Hettie, to find out what it is! I hope you have all made your costumes? If you haven't, it's a bit late now.'

'Costumes?' I ask Joel.'

The Hallowe'en party,' he says. 'It's tonight. Had you forgotten? How can you forget that? I'm going as a zombie.'

He goes cross-eyed, stretches his mouth and lurches towards me. I shrug him off and see a hurt look come to his face.

'What?' he says.

I can't tell him what. How can I tell him it seems stupid and childish? Dressing up, throwing around fake blood, pretending to be ghosts and zombies, when I am dealing with the real thing?

'Nothing,' I mutter. 'I'm just tired.'

'Zac! Can I talk to you for a minute?'

Mr Carter is waving at me.'

'I'll catch you up, yeah?'

Joel heads off with Jamie. Jamie is walking like The Mummy. He takes Joel in a headlock as they go.

Mr Carter closes the door behind them.

'I am so relieved to see you,' he says. 'I had *no idea* what you were doing last night. If I had, I would never have let you go.'

'Did Grampy tell you?'

He nods. 'I took him home then sat with him for a while, till I was sure he was okay. He told me everything. I couldn't believe what I was hearing. Talk about dangerous, Zac! So what happened? Did you find them?'

I tell him about Nic Bell. The colour drains from

his face.

'It must have been the ammonia,' he says.

'What?'

'The ammonia in the … cow waste. Zombie bodies must have a different chemical make-up to us. That's why he reacted so badly to it.'

'*Reacted so badly?* He melted like wax, right in front of me. And it was my fault.'

'No, no, Zac. 'Fault' is not the right word here. He was chasing you and something happened to him as a result. There is nothing to feel guilty about.

It seems to me some jobs are all about life and death. What your grandfather is doing - what you are now doing - is one of those jobs. You're keeping the living safe from the dead.'

'I'm eleven years old.'

'That makes you even more remarkable.' He sighs and reaches for his jacket then stops, as if he's had a sudden thought.

'What about his brothers? Did they see this happen?'

'No. He was alone.'

'So they must have known you were following, and left him behind to deal with you?'

I can't see where Mr Carter is going with this, but I am starting to get A Very Bad Feeling.

'What are you saying?'

'Oh, it's nothing.'

'Tell me.'

'It's nothing, really. When Nic doesn't return, they won't know what happened to him…'

'... but they will know *something* happened, and they will know who he was with last?'

Mr Carter says nothing.

Then I know, this is *really* bad.

CHAPTER 15

I arrive home from school mega-hungry. My brain is doing so much thinking this week, I seem to be hungry all the time. I let myself in, hoping to catch the smell of something good cooking, but am disappointed.

Mum's in the kitchen, eating a sandwich and a family-size bag of crisps.

'Grampy asked if you can spend the night round there again,' she says. 'I said yes. Are you two planning something?'

I suddenly wonder if she knows what we're up to. Did *she* ever do it? She is Grampy's daughter, after all.

I decide to ask Grampy, not Mum. I still don't know how secret this ghost work is.

'No, we just watch tv,' I say. 'Can I have something to eat?'

'Grampy's cooking for you.'

'That will take forever! I could eat a donkey.'

'Oh, you poor, starving child,' she says theatrically. '*Bad* mummy!'

She pushes the crisps across the table towards me. 'Eat. And you can make your own sandwich. You're not having mine!'

I go to the fridge and pull out margarine, cheese and a jar of pickle. Then I get the bread.

'Mum?' I say, as I make the sandwich. 'How do

you manage to be so brave?'

'Brave? You think I'm brave?'

'Yes. You deal with all kinds of horrible things. Bad people who've hurt their pets. Don't you get scared sometimes?'

She nods as she chews.

'Sometimes people come to the centre *really* angry. We have their dog, 'cause they've been mistreating it, but they are still demanding we give it back. They're shouting, smashing things, threatening to punch us. That can get scary.

But at the time, there's so much going on, I don't really think about it. It's *afterwards* I feel it. Sometimes I get so shaky, I have to go to the staffroom to calm down. I'll have a cup of tea. Eat half a packet of biscuits! It's the adrenaline. It pumps round your body when you're in trouble and then, when it's over, it makes you shake.'

'But you could train yourself to be brave, if you wanted to?'

Mum reaches for the crisps again.

'Could I? I don't know! You'd need to ask a soldier that. They must have training. But I bet they'd say they get scared too, and the training just enables them do their job under extreme pressure. We all get scared, Zac. We can't help it. Most people who are 'brave' don't feel brave at the time. They're just getting on with it. Doing what has to be done.Anyway, where has this come from?'

I join her at the table. 'It's homework. We're writing ghost stories. I want my character to be brave.'

She smiles. 'Anyone can be brave in a story. That's why I love books! Stories are so much easier than real life.'

CHAPTER 16

Grampy totally shocks me. When I get round to his house, I find he's cooked a beef stew with dumplings, carrots, mashed potatoes - the lot. The smell in his kitchen would make a dog drool. It's like a five-star restaurant.

'Sit down, lad,' he says. 'I'll dish up.'

'What's all this for?'

'Big night ahead,' he says. 'Lots to do. This will keep out the cold. Give us energy.'

He's spooning out the stew now. Thick gravy, fluffy dumplings... But my appetite has vanished. I *want* to be the big hero. *Want* to be fighting and winning like people in the movies. But the truth is, it's scary hunting zombeards. You're not in control, there's something out to get you, and you can die doing it.

'Tuck in, Zac!'

I try to think of other things while I eat. Grampy's right, I will need something to keep me going.

'Grampy - does Mum know what we're doing?'

'No,' he says, 'and I think it's best it stays that way.'

'But she's your daughter. Didn't you train her, when she was my age? To do this work?'

I take another mouthful of food. It's so good! Fear or not, I'm falling in love with this stew.

'No,' says Grampy, his mouth half-full of

dumpling. 'I wanted to, but your Nana was dead set against it. *Girls don't do that kind of thing, Bill,* she said. *It's up to you boys to protect us.*

Can you imagine someone saying that these days? There'd be such trouble! But they were different times. So we agreed we'd wait until your Auntie Kim grew a bit older, and then see.'

'You trained *Auntie Kim?*'

'Yes. Your Nana changed her mind. Kim had so much energy… She needed something in her life that would challenge her. And she was good, *really* good. She was strong and clever. Quick to learn. Fearless! We had many adventures together. The Challenge of the Disappearing Coffins sticks in my mind! But then she decided she didn't want to do it anymore.'

'Why?'

Grampy smiles. 'Too old.'

'What?'

'There came a time when she wanted to be out with her mates at night, not creeping round graveyards with me. You'll probably be the same!' He chuckles like Santa. 'I hope you stick with the work though. I think you can be better than Kim.'

'Really?' I am amazed. Auntie Kim is one of my heroes. She's always doing amazing things.

'Really.'

I'm so pleased with this thought, I clean my plate and ask for more.

CHAPTER 17

At six o'clock we button up our coats and leave the house, heading for the graveyard. Grampy has promised to tell me the plan as we walk.

It's dark and the streets are busy with little kids Trick or Treating. Ghosts, witches, vampires, zombies, mummies… They all come down the street towards us, along with a Spiderman, two Darth Vaders and a glittery princess. Some people just don't get Hallowe'en.

The little kids are with parents, but there are bigger ones on their own, heading to school for the Hallowe'en party. Ethan Lloyd comes along the road, dressed in his normal clothes but with a massive **?** pinned to his front.

'You're goin' the wrong way, boy,' he says as he draws near.

Ethan is in my class. He's from Wales and always says *boy*.

'Party's that way. And where's your costume?'

'I was going to ask you that,' I say. 'What's this?' The question mark is held on with a safety pin. I flip it up and down like a cat flap.

'Isn't it obvious?'

'No.'

'Guess, boy.'

'Are you the Riddler from Batman?'

'No.'

'Then I have no idea.'

'Think of a question,' he says, waving his hand to encourage me. 'There's a clue for you.'

'No. Still don't know.'

He grins an almighty grin. 'I'm a Which,' he says. 'A Which, boy!'

'*Ohhhhh…!* I get it now. But I'm not coming, Ethan. That's why I'm not dressed. Gotta do some things with my Grampy. Look, I'd better go. Have a good one.'

I race up the street to catch my grandad.

'He's a strange lad, that one,' says Grampy. 'But I like him.'

'It's hard not to,' I say. We walk on.

'Grampy, I have a question. It's about the zombeards' breathing. I know they do it. I heard Nic Bell panting. But why do they need to breathe if they are dead?'

'Good question,' says Grampy. 'I confess I don't know the answer. I reckon it's like the cricket - it's habit. They do it because they always have. Same with blinking or eating. Does that make sense?'

'Yes.'

We turn into Mermaid Lane and I remember Grampy's promise.

'What's the plan?'

Grampy blows his nose loudly. 'We need to get Shannon back. That's the most important thing. These fellas never come out in the day. They stay in their cave till it's dark. But even then, they don't come out until late. Ten o'clock is the earliest they've been seen. I reckon they sleep till then.

So first we go to the shed in the graveyard. Get some equipment. Then we head to the beach. We'll try to get Shannon before they wake up.'

I stop dead in the lane. 'Are you saying we're just going to walk in there? Into their cave?'

'That's the plan.'

'But…'

Grampy's not listening. He marches on, pulling his scarf up tighter to his ears. How can I tell him how I feel about this? How I hate small spaces? How I feel trapped, start to panic, can't think, can't breathe?

He expects me to go into a cave? In the dark? With zombies?

Oh Grampy. I hope the equipment's good.

As we near the graveyard, we hear a girl screaming. *Shannon?* We speed up. My heart is hammering already. But it's just a gang of older kids from the high school, messing round for Hallowe'en. One of the girls is being chased by a lad in a clown mask.

'Hope they move on soon,' mutters Grampy. 'It's really not the night to be here.'

One of the lads calls over to us as we go up the main path: 'The church is locked!'

'No matter,' Grampy replies. 'We're just passing through.'

He turns left, like we're going to the gate I used last night. But instead, he leads me round the back of the church and over to a large shed in the corner of the graveyard. It's under a yew tree, so it's well hidden. I've never noticed it before.

He pulls a torch out of his pocket and switches it on, then pulls out a key and slips it into the padlock on the shed door. *Clllk*. He takes off the lock and opens the door.He goes into the shed. I peer in. He's picking up shovels, garden forks, shears.

'Where's the equipment?'

'We'll have to be creative, lad. Use what we have.'

'But… *Grampy?!*'

'What? Did you think it was going to be like James Bond?'

YES, I want to say, I was expecting a secret stash of weapons, all high-tech, high-military stuff. I thought we were going to be strapping it on, layer after layer, with body armour and night-vision goggles. Instead, we are hunting zombies with a torch and a garden fork?

'I have some gear left,' says Grampy. 'The Blaster. The warning buttons. A few bits and bobs. Your Auntie Kim still helps out with things like that, keeping them going. But it was the government, Zac. They cut the funding, years ago. Said there hadn't been any trouble so there was no need to keep funding the Unit. Damn fools couldn't see there had been no trouble *because* of the Unit. Here - take this.'

He hands me a bottle of washing-up liquid. But when I squeeze it, there's no liquid inside. Dark powder comes out.

'What is it?'

'A mixture of pepper, chilli and mustard powder. It's a bit like the Brassica Juice, but easier to carry. It won't kill them, but it will stop them for a moment. And a moment can make all the difference.'

'Does it sting their eyes?'

'Yes, hot and fierce. But it will sting yours too, so make sure you aim it well. And take the top completely off before you do it. You need a wide hole, not that little one.'

Grampy is stuffing packets and bottles into his pockets. From a peg on the wall, he takes down a savage-looking blade with jagged edges. I guess it's used for sawing off branches. I don't know what he's planning to saw off tonight.

'Ready?'

'Ready.'

CHAPTER 18

We leave the graveyard through the side gate and head towards the fields, along the same path I followed last night. Spyker appears and follows us. When we get to the end, we take the path towards the sea, not the one to Cold Wall Farm. Spyker comes no further.

We walk through the cabbages. The sky has cleared. The moon is hanging heavy and nearly-full. It means we can see, but things can see us too.

Thin strips of cloud skim across it. It's a perfect Hallowe'en moon.

We reach the clifftop path. It's weird - I've lived here all my life, but the sight of the sea can still take my breath away. It is gorgeous tonight, shimmering like fish scales, silver in the moonlight. The night is calm and still. Cold. The air smells of salt and danger.

Far behind us, the church clock strikes the hour. Seven o'clock already? A picture leaps into my head: Anderson and Jaden Bell, fast asleep. I hope they stay that way.

There's a rough track that leads down to the beach. It shines chalky-white in the moonlight. We go down, down, down to the beach. The sea is halfway in, the low waves breaking on the beach with soft sighs.

Everything seems quiet, calm, watchful. It's as if

the whole world is waiting to see what comes next.

I'm starting to feel sick. It's my nerves. I'm sorry I ate so much stew.We walk along the beach close by the cliffs, not down the middle, but still I feel I'm going to brown my pants. There is nowhere to hide. *Nowhere.* The chalky cliffs are bouncing the moonlight back. It's ridiculously bright.

Grampy starts to slow down. Then he stops, puts his finger to his lips and points: *in there.*

I see an opening in the cliff wall, no more than a slit. Oh. My. Jumping. Monkeys. There is no way I want to go in there, but I still haven't told him. He fishes inside one of the many pockets in his coat and pulls out a second torch. He hands it to me.

'Can I use this, in there?' I mouth, like I'm in some black and white silent movie. Grampy rocks his hand from side to side: *maybe.* His lips form silent words: 'Be careful.'

He leans in close and whispers into my ear. 'I will go in alone and try to find Shannon. You wait here. Keep your eyes and ears open.'

He slips into the cave opening. I don't know if this is better or worse. I'm not in the cave, but now I'm alone.

My mind flashes back to Nic Bell. The escape across the field and the melting muck heap. I close my eyes. Try to blink the memory away. *What am I doing?* I say to myself. *I should be at the party with Jamie and Ethan and the rest of them. Playing at being zombies, not fighting them for real.*

I open my eyes. Look at my watch. 7.35. What time did Grampy go in? I didn't look.

I take a deep breath, trying to calm the churning in my stomach. I pull the washing-up bottle out of my pocket and pull off the top. That calms me down a bit.

I look up the beach. There's nothing moving. I look down the beach. There's -- someone coming. Baggy jeans. Puffy jacket. Baseball cap. Rolling swagger, like he's on the deck of a ship.

It's Jaden Bell - and he's seen me.

He starts to run.I want to run too, but my legs won't work. I've shut down.

Run. *Run!*His eyes are amber, super-bright. His beard hangs like a bib, black, black, black. It's like Nic Bell all over again, except there's no farm to run to this time.

Then a cry cuts through the night air. *Grampy?* The spell is broken. My legs move.

I dive into the cave.

CHAPTER 19

Whoa, it's dark. Just a slice of light where the moon comes in through the opening. But some inner voice tells me: *don't turn on the torch, hide in the shadows.* So I flatten myself against the dark wall and pray my drumming heart won't give me away.

It doesn't.

Jaden Bell comes lumbering in, fists curled. He stands in the shaft of moonlight, his head swivelling from side to side. He sniffs the air like a dog, but that mustn't work, because he doesn't find me. He heads deeper into the cave and leaves me behind.

I hear the cry again, then a roar and a groan. I want to help Grampy, but it's dark. The cave is closing in.

Breathe, I tell myself. *Breathe. Pretend it's a computer game. Zombie Beach. Begin.*

I shine my torch directly down, so I can see just a step or two in front. Step by step, one foot after another, I follow Jaden.

The cave goes back… and back… and back. Deeper and deeper into the cliff. Soon the moonlight is far behind me, and there is still no sign of Grampy. The sound of the sea is deafening. The cave is amplifying the sound. It sounds like there's a storm outside, though I know there isn't.

I can't hear any more cries.

I creep forward and find the cave splits into two tunnels. *No!* I have no idea which one to choose. Left? Right? Left? I tilt my head, trying to catch any sound.

Nothing.

I choose Right. It's wider than Left.

I carry on. I can't believe I'm doing this. The tunnel gets wetter. Drips from the roof fall on to my face. I can't wipe them away. My left hand has the torch, my right is in my pocket, holding onto the pepper spray. Deeper… Deeper…

FFFFFFFFF! I spin around, drop the torch and squeeze the pepper spray with both hands, full force, as something comes at me from behind. The pepper shoots out and hits Jaden Bell right in the face. He howls in pain. I grab the torch from the floor, turn and run.

The tunnel goes on forever, an endless tube of black, like I'm running through a worm. I bang against the wall sides but keep going. I stumble but keep going. I think my lungs are going to explode but I keep going. Because Jaden Bell is coming, coming, coming.

The tunnel starts to climb. Now it's like running uphill. It's killing me, but I have to keep going. Up and up and up and up and up and up and up and up.

Then ahead, in the wild, bouncing torchlight, I see a flight of steps. I scramble up, but there's a trap door at the end of them. It's heavy wood. I can't budge it. I'm caught like a rat in a drainpipe. I put my back against the door and try to force it upwards. It won't move. I put down the torch and pepper spray and hammer with my fists.

'LET ME OUT! SOMEONE! LET ME OUT!'

But the only reply comes from Jaden Bell. It echoes along the dark tunnel: 'I'm coming to get you. I'm coming to get you...'

I take up the pepper spray again. It's still half-full. I hold it in front of me like some kind of Ninja warrior blade. If I'm gonna die, I'll go down fighting.

I close my eyes, breathe deep, gather my energy, calm my nerves and concentrate. Right now I might be a desperate kid, facing death with a washing-up liquid bottle, but I have never felt more alive. And you know what? I can feel my courage. My determination. My strength.

*I can do this.*I open my eyes, face the darkness once more - and the trapdoor opens.

I look up. There's a ghost looking down at me.

'Come.'

CHAPTER 20

I clamber up on all fours and come out - into the church? I wasn't expecting *that*. I collapse onto a cold stone floor for a second. When I open my eyes, I find a ring of ghosts around me, peering down.

'You need to go,' says a hissy voice. Spyker! 'We cannot stop the bearded one. He will be too strong for us.'

'But my Grampy is still down there!'

'You cannot help him if you are dead.'

I stagger to my feet, the ghosts falling back. One of them beckons me to follow. He leads me through the church to a small side door. On the wall beside it there is a key, hanging from a hook.

'Open it,' he says, in a wispy voice. 'I cannot.'

I open the door and step out into the chilly night.

'Thank you,' I say.

He nods, then looks over his shoulder. When he turns back, his face shows his distress. 'Go. He's coming.'

I stumble off down the path. The graveyard is deserted now, the older kids have gone. I go through the main gate and turn for home.

My head is spinning like a tumble dryer. How did I come out in the church? Oh - the smugglers' tunnels! So that story is true after all.

But what about GRAMPY? Is he alright? Why did he cry out like that? Should I go back to him?

No - I'll go home and tell Mum. She'll know what to do.

I jog home, because Jaden Bell must be out of the church and on my trail by now. I have never run so far, so fast as I have run tonight. I will be fit enough for a marathon after this. If I survive.

Into the town, up our road… The little kids are in bed now. The road is empty. I reach our house - there's no light on. *What?* I ring the doorbell. No answer. *Mum?* I ring again, longer this time. Still nothing. I dig in my pocket for my key - I don't have it. I must have left it on the kitchen table earlier. *No!*

I look down the road to see if Jaden is coming. No sign. I ring the bell again.

Then I remember - Mum has gone to the cinema. She told me as I left the house. *No!*

Who else is there, with Grampy gone? The police? No. Then who…

MR CARTER! *Yes!* I punch the air and do a happy dance. He will know what to do.

I start running to school. To the Hallowe'en party.

CHAPTER 21

The school hall is packed. Everyone is dancing to *The Monster Mash.* Even the Head, Mrs Hannan, is on the dance floor. She's dressed like Professor McGonagall from Harry Potter. Mrs Wachowski is a witch. Mr Dunn is Frankenstein's monster. Miss Taylor is a cat, with black ears and a long tail. But where is Mr Carter?

I walk around the edge of the dance floor, trying to peer over heads.

Aargh! Ethan grabs me from behind. He shouts over the loud music: 'You change your mind, boy?'

'Kind of. I'm looking for Mr Carter.'

'Ah - Dracula! He is here. Somewhere. Oh, I remember. He's doing the bar.'

I nod and move on. It won't be a real bar. Just fruit 'mocktails.' Yeah, I get there and it's full of signs for Bat's Blood, Vampire Vodka and Werewolf Whisky. Is that allowed? Even if it's not real? I bet someone will complain.

Where is Mr Carter?

Miss Kapoor is serving. She is dressed as a mummy, but her bandages are coming undone. The one on her wrist dangles in the cups as she serves. She is soaked with Bat's Blood.

I lean over the bar and shout: 'I am looking for Mr Carter?'

'Outside,' she shouts back. 'He said he needed

fresh air.'

I head for the door. But as I do, I see someone coming across the dance floor. Weaving in and out of the dancers, coming right for me, and no one is stopping him because he looks like a zombie. Because he *is* a zombie.

I run.

I burst through the front doors and back into the chill of the night. *Where is Mr Carter?* Is he round the back? Why? Does he smoke or something?

I run round the back of the building. As I do, I hear the front doors slam, like something has crashed through them.

It's dark back here and quieter. I hear a low voice. There's a figure up ahead in a long black cape.

'Mr Carter!'

He turns. His face is vampire white. Fake blood drips from the corners of his mouth. Dracula.

'Gotta go,' he says into his phone and puts it away. 'Zac, what's -'

He says no more, because Jaden Bell crashes round the corner, and I have never seen anything looking angrier. His eyes are red-raw, still wet with stinging tears.

'Found you,' he says. His voice is grave-dirt rough. He comes towards us.

Mr Carter pushes me behind him.

'Back off,' he says.

Jaden laughs. 'Never listened to no teacher man

when I was alive. Not gonna start now.' He comes closer. 'I want the boy. You can go.'

'No,' says Mr C. 'You have to come through me.'

There's a pause. They're like cats on a roof, facing off. Then it all happens so fast.

Jaden springs forward and I push Mr C aside, because this is my problem, not his. And I do the only thing I can think of: I grab hold of Jaden's beard and pull. HARD.

It comes off in my hand, with a flap of skin still attached. I throw it down.

Jaden gasps - an almighty gasp, like he's dragging it up from the soles of his feet. He looks for his beard. It's on the floor like a dead animal. He starts to sway on his feet. His eyes fix on me with a look of disbelief. Then he begins to crumble. He crumbles like cheese, falling to pieces in front of our eyes.

'What the - ' cries Mr C, and he starts forward.

'Don't touch him!' I cry, like I'm some sort of expert now. I grab hold of Mr Carter's sleeve and pull him back. I'm so sure this is the right thing to do.

We watch, unable not to, as Jaden Bell disappears in front of our eyes, the bits seeming to sink into the ground, back into the grave he crawled out from.

But the beard is still there on the ground, a scrap of black fur on a flap of skin. Mr Carter moves closer. He bends down and peers at it before I can stop him.

'No!'

I pull him back again, but it's too late. The beard leaps from the ground like a rat and lands on his chest. It hangs on and starts to crawl up towards his face.

And something tells me - no SCREAMS at me - *if that reaches his chin, he will become a zombeard too.*

Mr Carter is frantic now: 'Get it off! Get it off me!'

He's clawing at it, pulling with all his strength, but the unearthly beard is holding on, crawling up his chest, centimetre by centimetre.

I am pulling it too now, but it's not helping. I don't know what else I can do.

'In my pocket!' Mr C cries suddenly. 'My lighter! In my jacket pocket! Burn it, Zac! Burn it!'

I reach into his pocket, fingers fishing. I find the lighter! Pull it out, click it, put it to the beard.

Eeeeeeeeeeeeeeeeeeeeeeeeee!

The beard squeals like a devil, falls to the floor and starts thrashing around. There are sparks flying everywhere - it's like a firework. Then it sizzles to a stop, all burnt up, and there's nothing left except the sickly-sweet smell of burnt hair.

Mr Carter seems to fold in on himself. He's on his hands and knees, taking great gulping breaths of air.

I don't blame him. He came so close. *So close.*

We both did.

Suddenly I remember why I am looking for him.

'My Grampy,' I say. 'He's down in the tunnels with Anderson Bell. I think he's dead.'

'What?'

'Grampy. I had to leave him.'

Mr Carter struggles to his feet and stares at me.

'What?'

'Tonight. We went to the beach. The zombeards have a cave. He went in on his own. I heard a cry, but Jaden Bell came for me. I couldn't stay. I came through the tunnel.'

'The tunnel?'

'From the beach to the church. The smugglers' tunnel.'

Mr Carter shakes his head as he tries to take it all in.

'We have to go down there,' he says at last, but I can see the fear on his face. 'Can we get in from the beach?'

'I don't think so. The tide was coming in.'

'Can we get in from the church?'

'Maybe. The ghosts would let us back down but...' The memory of the tunnel comes back to me, hard.

He sees and nods. 'I know. I don't want to go that way either. A tunnel sounds too confined. Too tight, like a trap. But I can't see any other way.'

Neither can I.

CHAPTER 22

We walk to the church in silence, me and a man dressed as Dracula. What is there to say?

Spyker is sitting on the church wall as we approach. Mr Carter's eyes grow wide when he sees him.

'Can you let us back down, Spyker?'

'Yesss,' he hisses. 'But is that wise?'

'We have no choice. Have you seen Anderson Bell tonight?'

'No.'

'Then he must still be down in the cave. With Grampy.'

Spyker jumps from the wall and pads up the path in front of us. He leads us to the side door, the one I came out of. It's still open.

A huddle of ghosts are in there - the one who let me out earlier, the one called Jonathan and a few more, including two women and a little girl. Their eyes are silver-grey.

I had wondered how they got the trapdoor open, since they don't seem able to touch anything. Now I see the door has a heavy brass ring set into it, and there's a rope attached. Spyker, who isn't a ghost but very much real, must have opened it earlier.

But now it's Mr Carter who takes hold of the ring and lifts the door up.

'Go well,' says the ghost called Jonathan.

We descend into the darkness.

Down the steps and along the tunnel we go. Mr C takes the torch and leads the way. I follow behind, trying not to panic at the thought of being in a tunnel. Again.

We walk for ages, then I whisper 'Wait,' slip in front and take the torch. Something tells me we're getting close. I don't want Mr C bursting in.

And I know - he's the Grown Up, and a teacher, and I'm only a kid, but it feels right to me. What did Grampy say? *You have Morgan blood in your veins.* I am starting to understand what that means. Starting to believe this *is* the work for me. I seem to know what needs to be done, without having to think. That feels weird but amazing too. I don't think I've ever felt so sure, even though I'm wide-eye scared. And I *am* scared. It wouldn't be safe if I wasn't. I could do stupid things. Fear makes you sharp.

So I go in front and we slow down. I was right - very soon we reach the fork in the tunnel. I point and mouth: '*This way.*' Mr C nods.

We creep up this new bit of tunnel. It's silly dark. I have my hand over the torchlight, so just the tiniest bit of light shines through. But even then, it will be enough to alert Anderson if he's here. But what else can I do? Turn it off and it will be so dark, only a bat could see.

One foot in front of the other, on we go. My ears

are straining for any sound. My nose is tasting the air. There's nothing but salt and dampness.

Then I kick something and nearly fall. It groans.

Grampy?

He struggles to sit up. There's blood on his face. One eye is closed.

'Zac...'

'Don't speak, Grampy! We need to go. Can you stand?'

I get hold of his arm to help - and then I see something. A shape in the darkness. I flick up the torchlight. It's Shannon. She's standing there, not moving, not seeing. Her eyes screw up as the light hits. My hearts tears at the sight of her. But what can I do?

Mr C helps me pull Grampy to his feet. But as we do, Shannon's head turns. It swivels like an owl's, right round on her neck, and she looks up into the far tunnel.

'Anderson is coming,' says Mr C.

CHAPTER 23

'We must go.'

Mr Carter and I do our best, but Grampy can barely walk. Every step is an effort. We hold him between us, one on either side.

'Come on,' I say, under my breath.

'Come on, come on.' I don't want to sound impatient but every second is counting here.

We head back towards the cave and the beach - it's our only chance. There's no way Grampy will make it back to the church through the tunnel.

Then Mr Carter stops and turns. 'Oh dear heavens -'

And before he can say or do anything more, Anderson is upon us. He grabs Mr C and throws him aside like he's a doll. Grampy collapses. Then Anderson looks straight at me, his eyes dancing, and I know this is what he *really* wants. To get *me,* as revenge for his brother Nic.

I run. Again. As fast as I can, into the darkness. Anderson follows. He's howling and laughing like they do in the movies. I think my heart is going to stop beating. I have never heard anything so scary in all my life.

I reach the cave - suddenly there's light. I keep on running, through the opening and out onto the beach.

The night is blue with moonlight. It's gorgeous.

I don't know how I see that, but I do. It must be because I'm alive to everything, all my senses working overtime.

Anderson hurls himself out of the cave behind me. I see how big he is. How strong. His beard hangs down to his waist, filthier than ever. He lunges towards me and I have no weapon and nowhere to go. The tide has come in, there's just a scrap of beach. I am cut off from the rest of it.

The sea.

It's that something in my head, shouting again. *GO INTO THE SEA.*

I throw off my jacket, kick off my boots and head for the dark water. I'm a good swimmer. I can do this. I *have* to do this.

Aiee, it's cold. I wade out as far as I can, till the water is up to my chest, then I turn and shout to Anderson. He's standing at the tideline like a toddler, backing off whenever a wave rolls in.

'You want me, Anderson? Then come and get me.'

He pulls back as another wave breaks. It's a tiny one. The sea is calm tonight.

'Come *on,* baby boy.'

Why am I taunting him? I don't know, but it feels right.

Anderson says something, but the sea breeze carries it away. He starts pacing up and down, looking at me, like a dog that's deciding whether or not to swim. I wonder how much brain power he has. Not much, it seems.

'Come *on*.'

He pulls off his coat and begins to wade into the water. He looks down as he does, like he doesn't quite understand what he's doing. He stops. Pulls off his boots. Begins to wade again.

I turn and start swimming, heading right out to sea. There's a buoy with a light flashing on it, far out but not too far out for a strong swimmer. I've swum there before. It's a safe-ish swim. Usually.

I stop after a minute, turn and tread water. Anderson isn't following. And suddenly I realise why I am doing this. It's what Grampy told me, nights ago. *Zombies drown. Their brains can't cope. They swallow water.*

I hope it works with zombeards too.

'Come on, Anderson. What'ya waiting for?'

His eyes narrow as he stares at me, then some part of his brain remembers a time when he could swim. He launches himself fully into the water and begins to swim.

And boy, can he swim.

I thought he would struggle and go under but he's coming at me surer than a shark. His body memory must be good.

I turn and swim for my life. I can't stop, I can't look back. I just aim for the buoy. I see the light flashing, every time I lift my head from the water.

Keep going, keep going, keep going...

But then my foot is grabbed and I'm pulled under the water hard and *I'm* the one swallowing water. It goes up my nose and into my mouth. I feel it go down into my lungs. I kick hard, break free and come up for air.

Anderson is right beside me. He dives at me. I manage to move and he lands with an almighty splash. But he rolls onto his back and comes upright again. He lunges again and again and again. Somehow I keep evading him. I'm like a dolphin tonight, slick-quick in the water.

I see the fury in his face and the frustration. His beard is wet as a rope, stuck to his chest. His eyes burn above it. But he's grunting hard. This is taking a lot of effort.

I splash him, like I splash Jamie in the swimming pool. His eyes close against the water. Does it sting? I splash him more. He falls backwards, his head dips under the waves, and he swallows a great mouthful of water. He comes back up coughing and spluttering. There's panic on his face now. He starts to gasp, and his body memory seems to fail him. He forgets how to tread water. It's like his brain can't cope with so many tasks at once. In struggling to breathe, he forgets how to swim.

His head goes under again. And again. And again. Every time he goes under, he swallows more. It's terrible to see. He's gasping and fighting for life - or whatever it is a zombie has.

Survival, I guess.

As it all gets too much, I head back to the beach. I swim and swim, then pull myself out of the water.

Grampy and Mr Carter are on the beach, watching. I turn and see Anderson go down under the water yet again. His hand comes up, out of the waves, fingers wide. It looks like a starfish, black against the deep blue sky. Then it sinks beneath the waves and he is gone.

CHAPTER 24

Mr Carter is holding my jacket. 'You'll freeze to death,' he says, handing it to me. 'Put it on.'

He's right. Suddenly I feel how cold the night is.

Grampy is sitting on the sand. Mr C helps him to his feet. 'Come on, let's get you home.'

'Wait,' I say. 'Give me the torch.'

'Zac -'

'Just give me the torch.' Mr C hands it over and I head for the cave. Slip inside, into the darkness again.

Where the tunnel forks, I choose Left. Shannon is still in there, where I last saw her.

She flinches as my torch finds her, but I don't think she sees me.

'Shannon, come with me.'

She doesn't respond. I take a few steps closer.

'Come with me, Shannon.'

Still nothing. It's terrible to see her like this.

'Shannon - please. I'm trying to help.'

Nothing. Her eyes are flat and dull.

I do the only thing I can think of. I take hold of her hand. It's cold, like touching a toad.

She doesn't pull away. Her head swings from side to side, like her brain can't cope. Does she even *have* a brain now? The zombeards did, but she isn't a zombeard. She's - oh, I don't know what she is. She's not right, that's for sure.

‘Come on,’ I say again. Then she swivels her head, like she did earlier, and looks right into my eyes. And just for a second, there seems to be something there. It’s that same look she gave me in the churchyard.

‘Come with me.’

She starts to walk.

It’s like leading a two year old. Slowly, slowly, we go down the tunnel, through the cave and out into the night.

Mr Carter is ready to go. He’s wrapped his Dracula cape around Grampy, who looks like he’s hardly with us.

‘Well done, Zac,’ he says. He means it. I can see it on his face.

We start walking. We’re *so* slow. Grampy is no better at walking than Shannon. My teeth are chattering in my head, but there’s nothing I can do. This will take as long as it takes.

We walk along the beach - there’s a tiny bit of beach right next to the cliffs. Don’t know why I didn’t see it before, but then, I did have other things on my mind, haha.

We climb up that long, white, winding path to the top of the cliffs. Across the cabbage fields and into the churchyard. The ghosts are waiting for us. When they see Shannon they clap their hands, though there’s no sound. Smile and welcome her. She looks at them but doesn’t seem to see them.

Jonathan steps forward. 'There are blankets in the church,' he says. 'Come. Get warm.'

We follow him into the church. Soon Grampy and I are wrapped in tartan picnic blankets. Mr Carter makes tea in the tiny church kitchen. I cradle the hot mug in my fingers and begin to feel warm at last.

Mr C finds a first aid kit and tends to Grampy's head wound. 'This time, old man, you are going to the hospital,' he says.

'Perhaps,' Grampy says. 'First we need to decide what to do with Shannon.'

She is standing in the corner of the kitchen like a museum dummy.

'She needs to be a ghost again,' I say. 'She was happy as a ghost. But how can we do that?'

'I have no idea,' says Grampy. 'I've never been in this situation before. Jonathan? Do you have any suggestions?'

The tall ghost shakes his head. 'I have never known this either.'

'Spyker?'

The cat-thing is perched on the back of my armchair. 'No.'

We fall silent.

'It's been quite a night,' says Mr Carter, trying to brighten the mood. 'What time is it now? Must be nearly dawn. I'll have to go soon. Vampires turn to dust in the morning light!'

He chuckles softly. But my brain starts to whirr like beetle wings.

'Light,' I say.

'What?' '

Light! Grampy - did you ever see the zombeards in the daylight?'

He shakes his head.

'Did any of you?'

No.

'Then maybe that's it,' I say. 'Maybe Shannon would turn to dust if she was exposed to sunlight? Like a vampire? And maybe, with her body gone, she would become a ghost again?'

No one answers. They are all thinking.

'It's risky,' says Jonathan at last. 'We don't know what will happen. What if it is painful and doesn't work?'

'It always looks painful in the movies,' says Mr C.

'That is the movies,' says Grampy. 'Everything has to be high drama. It *might* work.'

'What other choice is there?' I say to Jonathan. 'Look at her. What are you going to do with her? You will all return to your graves soon, won't you? Are you going to put her back in her grave too? She's not like you. She's not *anything* anymore.'

'It's a difficult call, 'says Grampy. 'We can't ask for her thoughts on the matter.'

Everyone goes quiet again. I think back to the graveyard that night, when Anderson pulled her out of the ground. How she screamed at him not to do it. How she found herself just for a moment and looked right at me.

If I don't help her now, that look will haunt me for the rest of my days.

I rise to my feet. 'She asked me to help her,' I say. 'I am going to help her.'

I take her by the hand and lead her out of the church.

CHAPTER 25

We stand together in the graveyard, me and this pale, silent woman.

It's still dark, but the world is lightening at the edges. The birds are waking up and starting to sing. I can smell the salt on the sea breeze. I breathe deep and squeeze Shannon's hand.

'It's going to be okay,' I say.

I know the sun rises in the east, so I take her to the eastern side of the church. There's a wooden bench, and we sit there together as the sky begins to brighten. First it turns from deepest indigo to kingfisher blue. Then the warmth creeps in - a peachy-pink blush, spreading across the face of the sky.

And a strange thing happens. As the sky gets lighter, Shannon seems to wake up. It's like she's coming out of a dream. She's still lost in her own world. But some expression comes back into her eyes. The grey scale slides away and I start to see blueness. She even appears to be breathing. And then she speaks! I wasn't expecting that. But she starts talking to herself.

'He kissed me,' she says. *'He kissed me, like I was some kind of Sleeping Beauty. Some freaky fairytale princess. A kiss to drag me into his world. He knew it would do that. He knew I didn't want to go. But still he did it.'*

The graveyard is getting really bright now. There's a soft warmth about the place, an orange glow. And suddenly a wide band of sunlight comes over the church wall. It's like a fan, cutting through the trees, so bright, so golden.

Shannon gasps. She has seen it. She stands up and begins walking. She leaves footprints in the grass as she goes. The morning frost is melting. She raises her arms and opens them wide, like she's hugging the morning - and steps into the fan of light.

I hold my breath and wait for a cry of pain. But it doesn't come. Instead I see a golden figure, and then she turns, and she is smiling. She smiles right at me. The old Shannon is back. Then she begins to sway on her feet and her body just disappears: *zoosh!* Like a magic trick. Her clothes fall to the ground, but she isn't in them. Then out from the pile of clothes comes her ghost, like a wisp of smoke. But it gets bigger and bigger, and she flies towards me, whooshes up and away over my head, then comes back over the churchyard and *zoosh!* She shoots down into her own grave.

I stand there gaping like a goldfish. Then I notice Mr Carter and Grampy by the church door. They saw it all too.

Their faces are a picture. Like they've just seen an angel.

Grampy turns to me. 'Lad,' he says wearily. 'It's time we were in our beds!'

CHAPTER 26

It's the next night. Grampy has been to the hospital and had his head checked. He will be fine, though he has a massive bruise and needed four stitches. Anderson Bell smacked him with a piece of wood. In the dark, Grampy never saw it coming.

I was able to get a long sleep today at Grampy's house. It is Saturday, so no school. I'm guessing Mr Carter has slept too. He is with us again, though no longer dressed as Dracula.

We are all heading to the church.

As soon as we arrive, the ghosts come to greet us. They are in a huddle, all smiling, then they part in the middle… and Shannon steps forward. She looks exactly how she was that night she was taken. Back in her grave clothes and happy.

'Thank you,' she says. 'Thank you all, so much.'

'Just doin' our job, Ma'am,' says Grampy in an American accent, and Shannon smiles even wider.

'And you,' she says, coming and standing in front of me, 'Zac. Extra-special thanks to you. If I could hug you, I would.'

I feel my face getting warm.

'Anyone would have done it,' I say.'No, I don't think that's true. They told me it was your idea to put me into sunlight?'

I nod. 'I am a bit proud of that.'

'And so you should be!' she laughs. 'And thank

you, Mr Carter. You have been wonderful.'

She blows him a kiss, and now his face is getting warm too. But I reckon it feels nice, all the same.

CHAPTER 27

Later, Grampy and I are alone in his house. Grampy has made hot chocolate and added a flake as a special treat.

'Here's to us, lad!' he says, raising his mug. 'Teamwork! You can't beat it.'

I sip my chocolate. It's sugar heaven.

'How do you feel about the work now?' he says, curiously. 'I know you were struggling a bit at the beginning.'

'Not only at the beginning,' I confess. 'The worst bit was Nic Bell. But with Jaden and Anderson, it was different. I didn't feel bad about them. And that worries me a bit. Because I did… finish them off.'

Grampy drinks his chocolate while he thinks.

'Don't feel bad about not feeling bad,' he says. 'You did what you had to do. And yes, it was hard and frightening and tough. You got cold and wet and worn out, and that's how it is, this work. But the rewards… *ah!* They make it worthwhile. Seeing Shannon in that pool of golden light… Well, it was like watching a fairy step out of a storybook.

That is the way to do this work, Zac. You focus on the good bits and put the bad to the back of your mind.'

I nod. That makes sense to me. It's been the hardest week of my life, for sure. I feel very tired.

But I feel older too. Like I've really grown up. I am stronger than I thought I was. I found my courage, down in that tunnel.

'So,' says Grampy. 'What do you think? Do you want more adventures like this?'

I don't need to think. 'Yes,' I say, with a grin. *'Bring 'em on.'*

Also by Cat Weatherill

Wild Magic

When a beautiful stranger comes to town,
Marianna follows him into a world of wild magic.
Soon she is alone and being stalked by a fearsome beast who needs someone to break a centuries-old curse.
But the price of breaking the curse is a terrible one…

An ancient spell, a spirited heroine and a desperate villain clash in a fast-moving adventure, full of unexpected enchantment and danger.

Don't miss reading this book. Like the Piper's tune, it is so real you can taste it – **GoodReads**

Also by Cat Weatherill

Barkbelly

Barkbelly has always been an outsider in the village,
and now a terrible accident means he
has to run away to save his life.

From the glitter of Carmenero's Circus to the pirate ship Mermaid and an island at the edge of the world, Barkbelly follows his dreams. But will they come true when he gets there?

'Glorious... A beautiful and touching story' – **The Observer**

Also by Cat Weatherill

Snowbone

The adventure continues as Snowbone fights against the slavery of her people. An exploding volcano, a strange prophesy, man-eating plants and a hero who flies without wings - they're all here, in a second whirlwind adventure set in the world of Ashenpeakers.

'A dazzling book, inventive in plot and rich in language'
- Carousel